The Rainbow Mystery

by Jennifer Dussling
illustrated by Barry Gott

Kane Press
New York

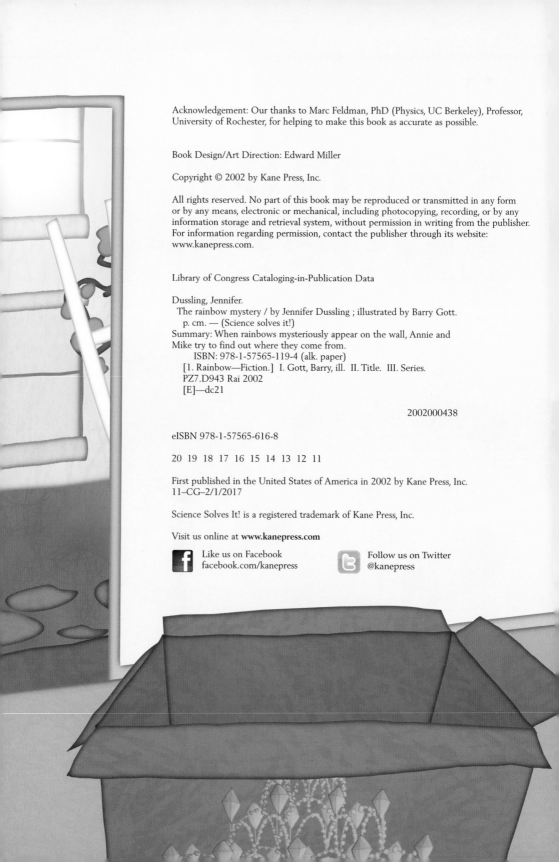

Acknowledgement: Our thanks to Marc Feldman, PhD (Physics, UC Berkeley), Professor, University of Rochester, for helping to make this book as accurate as possible.

Book Design/Art Direction: Edward Miller

Library of Congress Cataloging-in-Publication Data

Dussling, Jennifer.
  The rainbow mystery / by Jennifer Dussling ; illustrated by Barry Gott.
    p. cm. — (Science solves it!)
Summary: When rainbows mysteriously appear on the wall, Annie and Mike try to find out where they come from.
    ISBN: 978-1-57565-119-4 (alk. paper)
    [1. Rainbow—Fiction.] I. Gott, Barry, ill. II. Title. III. Series.
    PZ7.D943 Rai 2002
    [E]—dc21

                                                                    2002000438

eISBN 978-1-57565-616-8

20 19 18 17 16 15 14 13 12 11

First published in the United States of America in 2002 by Kane Press, Inc.
11–CG–2/1/2017

Science Solves It! is a registered trademark of Kane Press, Inc.

Visit us online at **www.kanepress.com**

Like us on Facebook
facebook.com/kanepress

Follow us on Twitter
@kanepress

Have you ever wanted to be a detective?
It's not easy. I know. I tried to solve a mystery
once. A rainbow mystery.

I was in the family room with my friend,
Mike. Mike never says much. Mom says that's
why I like him. I'm loud. Mike is quiet. I talk.
He listens.

We were making a fort from a big box. Mike had found the box by the house next door.

He was cutting out a window. I was telling him what to do. That's when I saw them— hundreds of little rainbows!

"Mike, look!" I yelled.

Mike looked. He almost fell over. The little rainbows danced across the wall. "Wow," was all he said.

We watched the rainbows. They faded away. Then they were gone. We jumped up and ran outside.

"No rain," said Mike.

I knew what he meant. Everyone knows rainbows come when it rains. But it wasn't raining.

How could there be a rainbow without rain?

I started thinking. "One time I saw a rainbow in a patch of oil," I said. "It wasn't raining then."

We looked. There was no patch of oil.

"Last summer I saw a rainbow in a sprinkler," I said. Was there a sprinkler nearby? No.

I remembered another time I saw a rainbow. My friend Kelly has a glass teardrop necklace. It makes a rainbow when the light hits it.

I didn't bother to look. I knew there were no glass teardrop necklaces around.

Mike and I sat down on the steps. It was late. The sun was low in the sky.

"We have to be detectives! We have to solve this mystery!" I said.

Mike nodded.

Mike came over real early the next morning. We sat like statues in the new fort. We waited and waited. No rainbows.

The day after that, Mike came for lunch. We waited in the fort again. Still no rainbows.

Monday was rainy. Mike thought for sure we would see the little rainbows again. But the rainbows didn't come.

On Tuesday Kelly wore her teardrop necklace to school. I didn't think the necklace would help. But I didn't have any other clues.

"Can you make a rainbow?" I asked her.

"I can try," Kelly said. She stood by the window and moved her necklace in the light.

"Look!" I yelled.

The teacher came over. He's a really nice guy. I showed him the rainbow.

"Terrific!" Mr. Royal said. He called the other kids over. "Kelly's necklace is like a prism," Mr. Royal told us. "A prism is a special piece of clear glass or plastic. It separates light into the seven rainbow colors."

A prism! Maybe a prism made the rainbows on the wall in my house!

Mr. Royal didn't say anything else about prisms. But he told us stuff about rainbows.

I wrote it all down.

Rainbow Stuff

An easy way to remember the Colors of the rainbow—they spell a name—

Roy G. Biv.

Red
Orange
Yellow
Green
Blue
Indigo
Violet

Indigo is just a fancy name for dark blue!

After school I told Mike about the necklace.

"It's a clue!" I said. "But I don't know enough about prisms." Mike nodded. He got a look in his eye. I knew what he was going to say.

"The library," he said.

So we went to the library and picked out a whole stack of books on rainbows and prisms.

The librarian was new. She smiled and turned
to the computer screen. "Look!" she said. "We're
neighbors! I'm Ms. Reed. I bought the house
next to yours. I moved in just last week."

She seemed nice. "I'm Annie. This is Mike,"
I said. Mike tugged on my sleeve. That meant
"hurry up!" He wanted to work on the mystery.

"Come visit sometime," Ms. Reed said.

"Okay," I told her.

I flopped on the couch with a fat book. I
started reading out loud. "A rainbow is made
when sunlight is bent by raindrops in the air.
A prism bends sunlight, too."

Mike said nothing. Instead, he gasped.

The rainbows were back!

I got up. I touched them. The rainbows showed on my fingers, too. All seven colors were there—red, orange, yellow, green, blue, indigo, and violet.

Then I thought of something. "What time is it?" I asked Mike.

Mike looked at his watch. "Five o'clock."

"Aha! It's the same time as before!" I said. "We didn't see the rainbows in the morning—or at noon. We only saw them after school!"

Mike nodded. "The sun," he said.

"Yes!" I said. I remembered this poster at school. "It must have to do with where the sun is."

Noon

Sunrise

Sunset

Like one person, we turned around and stared out the window.

"So, where is it?" Mike asked.

"I don't know," I said. "Let's go outside and look."

We rushed outside. No wonder we couldn't see the sun from the family room. It was behind the house next door.

"The answer to our mystery is in that house," I said.

Mike nodded.

At exactly 4:30 the next day, we rang the doorbell of Ms. Reed's house. "Annie! Mike!" she said. "You came for a visit! Come in."

We followed her inside. Before I could stop myself, the question burst out of me. "Ms. Reed, do you have a prism in your house?"

Ms. Reed looked puzzled. "A prism? No, I don't think so."

I was sad to hear that. But I didn't give up. Ms. Reed could have a prism and not know it.

She gave us lemonade and cookies. Then she asked if we'd like a tour of the house.

"Yes!" Mike and I said at the same instant.

Ms. Reed showed us the dining room. No prisms anywhere.

Then we went into the living room.
Still no prisms.

We took the stairs to the second floor.
The answer had to be up there!

"This is the music room," Ms. Reed said. She opened a door. "My favorite part is the chandelier. I just bought it."

I had no idea what a *shan-dow-leer* was—
maybe the fancy light on the ceiling. But I
didn't care. I was busy looking for prisms.
On the floor. In the cabinet. On the walls.
Then Mike grabbed my arm.

The sun had come out from behind a cloud.
Light streamed into the room. It hit the glass
chandelier. And rainbows danced on the wall
next to the window—just like in my family room!

I ran to the window. Yes! I could see into my house. I could see into the family room. I could see the rainbows on the wall, too!

For once I had nothing to say.

But Mike did.

"The glass chandelier is like a bunch of prisms!" he yelled. I stared at him. It was the longest sentence I'd ever heard him say.

"What do you mean?" Ms. Reed asked.

I told her the whole story—about the rainbows, and Kelly's necklace, and the library books. I even told her about making the fort from the big box Mike found outside.

"A big box?" Ms. Reed asked. "Was it by my house?"

"Yes," I said.

"The chandelier came in that box!" she said.

I looked at Mike. Mike looked at me. The
box! The biggest clue of all was in my house
the whole time.

Some detectives we were!

I can draw conclusions!

Me, too!

THINK LIKE A SCIENTIST

Mike and Annie think like scientists—and so can you!

Scientists are like detectives. They investigate. They look for clues and draw conclusions. A conclusion is what you learn from doing an investigation.

Look Back

On page 29, Mike says the longest sentence Annie has ever heard him say: "The glass chandelier is like a bunch of prisms!" Mike's sentence is also a conclusion: How did he come up with this conclusion? What clues did he use?

Try This!

You can make your own rainbow! You need:

- a clear plastic cup half full of water

- a flashlight

- a sheet of white paper

Carefully put the cup on a table or a counter so that about a third hangs over the edge. Hold the paper behind the cup while you shine the flashlight up through the bottom of it. What do you see? What conclusion can you draw?

Answers: Little rainbows on the paper! The water in the cup acts like a prism. It separates the light from the flashlight into rainbow colors.